Printed in the United States of America.

First Edition
1 3 5 7 9 10 8 6 4 2

This book is set in 18-point Berkeley.

Library of Congress Catalog Card Number: 00-100807
ISBN: 0-7868-4431-0 (paperback)
For more Disney Press fun, visit www.disneybooks.com

Adapted from the film
by Amy Edgar

New York

Chapter One

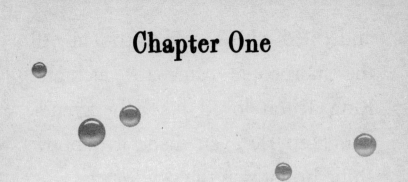

Not long ago, Ariel had given up being a mermaid to marry her true love, Prince Eric. Now they were expecting a baby!

Soon after Melody was born, Eric and Ariel sailed out to sea so Melody could meet her grandfather, King Triton. He was king of the seven seas, and ruled with a golden trident. All the merpeople came to celebrate. King Triton loved his baby granddaughter. He even made a rainbow shine brightly in the sky for her.

King Triton gave Melody a beautiful shell necklace with her name written on it. When he opened the shell pendant, out floated visions of life under the sea in Atlantica, the home of the merpeople. Lovely music played.

"My precious Melody," King Triton said, "I'm giving you this locket so you will never forget that part of your heart will always belong to the sea."

King Triton was about to place the locket around Melody's neck, when a giant black tentacle slithered out of the water and snatched the baby right out of Ariel's arms!

"Ursula's crazy sister!" shouted Sebastian, the old crab who served King Triton. Ursula's sister was named Morgana and was the ugliest, most evil creature in the ocean.

"Ursula would have simply *loved* to come," said Morgana. "But something came up. Oh yes, YOU ALL SHISH-KEBABBED HER!" She dangled Melody over the snapping jaws of her nasty sidekick, a huge tiger shark named Undertow. "Now, hand over the trident or your precious granddaughter will be shark chow!" cried Morgana.

Chapter Two

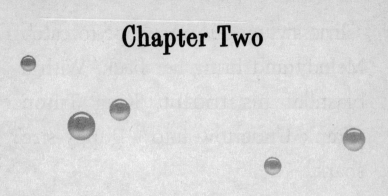

King Triton told Morgana that she could have anything she wanted, as long as she didn't harm Melody. Then, in a flash, Ariel grabbed Eric's sword and cut the ship's rigging. The boom flew around and struck Morgana, knocking her back and sending baby Melody flying.

Eric swung out on a rope to catch Melody and bring her back. With a blast of his trident, King Triton shrank Undertow into a guppy-size shark.

Morgana disappeared in a cloud of black ink. The king and his mermen took off after her.

Later, when Ariel and Eric were back at the beach, they were joined by King Triton, Sebastian, and Flounder.

"There's no sign of Morgana," King Triton said. "She's vanished."

"Until Morgana is found, Melody can't go in the sea," said Ariel. "And neither will I."

"But, *Ariel*!" cried Flounder.

"I'm sorry, Flounder, but if Morgana is anything like Ursula, she'll never give up. This is the only way. Melody can't know about merpeople or Atlantica or even you, Daddy."

"You're right," agreed King Triton sadly. "Sebastian, *you* will watch over Melody."

"Me? Baby-sit? Again?" Sebastian fell backward in shock.

King Triton took a long last look at his daughter and granddaughter. Then he swam away, dropping Melody's necklace into the sea.

Chapter Three

A tall brick wall surrounded the seaside castle. The wall stopped sea creatures from getting in and land creatures from getting out—or so Ariel and Eric thought. Inside the castle, music and the wonderful smells of a banquet were in the air. "Carlotta, have you seen Melody?" Ariel asked one of her servants. Fancy carriages were arriving outside.

Just beyond the wall, Sebastian paced back and forth. He muttered something about young girls. Then he dove in and caught up to Melody, who had slipped through the wall so she could go for a swim.

"Melody, it is expressly forbidden for you to be swimmin' beyond da safety of da seawall!" Sebastian reminded her. "Any such swimmin' is a reckless disregard of da rules!"

Melody ignored the old crab and kept swimming. What could be better than swimming in the sea? thought Melody. Happily, she picked up a pretty shell for her collection.

Then something else caught her eye. She swam down to take a closer look. It was a shell necklace.

"Melody, *please*. If your mother ever found out you've been swimming out here. . ." pleaded Sebastian.

"I know. I know. She'd flip. What's my mom got against the ocean, any-way?" asked Melody. "I mean, how could there be anything wrong with something so wonderful? You know, sometimes I even pretend I have *fins*!"

Suddenly, Melody remembered her birthday party back at the castle. She swam quickly home, slipped through a secret opening in the wall, and entered the castle through a window. She was dressing frantically when Ariel walked in. Neither of them noticed when Sebastian got caught in the bow of her dress.

Ariel smiled as she looked at her disheveled daughter. "Here, let me help," she said, picking up a brush.

"Mom, put down the brush. It's hopeless," said Melody. "Do I *have* to do this? Everybody thinks I'm weird."

"Oh, honey," said Ariel, "everyone has trouble fitting in at your age.

I know I did. I was a regular fish out of water."

"You? No way," said Melody with a sigh.

"Melody, is there something you want to talk about?" her mother asked. "You know you can always tell me anything."

Melody looked down. "Okay. What I dream about more than anything in the whole world . . ."

But before she could finish, they were interrupted by a knock at the door.

"Let's go, you two!" said Eric. "We can't keep three hundred people waiting!"

Promising they'd talk later, Ariel and Melody went downstairs to the party.

Chapter Four

The crowded ballroom glittered. The orchestra finished a beautiful piece of music. The noble people applauded politely.

Grimsby, the butler, stood stiffly at the top of the stairs and cleared his throat loudly. "May I present the Royal Highness, Princess Melody!"

Ariel, Eric, and their guests watched as Melody gracefully descended the staircase. They clapped when she reached the bottom. Melody smiled shyly at her young guests.

"If you ask me, she's a little strange," whispered one girl.

"I heard she actually talks to fish," said the boy next to her, with a giggle.

Just then a handsome boy walked over to Melody, smiled, and asked her to dance.

Slowly they started to spin around the room. Melody quickly forgot to be nervous. She was starting to enjoy herself when the boy screamed, "OWWWWWWW!"

Sebastian—still caught in Melody's bow—had clamped a sharp claw around one of his fingers. The boy shook the crab loose and sent him flying right into Chef Louis's cake.

"I'm so sorry," said Melody. "Are you okay, Sebastian?"

"*Who* is she talking to?" asked one of the guests.

"A *crab*!" laughed another guest.

Chef Louis wiped some frosting from his face and realized that Sebastian had ruined his cake. He took off after the crab with a big cleaver. He shouted, "YOU! You're goin' in the bouillabaisse!" Louis and Sebastian had never gotten along well.

The crowd erupted into laughter. In tears, Melody ran up to her room.

Chapter Five

In her room, Melody lay on her bed and sobbed.

"Sweetheart, I'm so sorry . . ." started Ariel.

"What's wrong with me?" wailed Melody.

Ariel tried to comfort her daughter. Melody picked up the necklace she'd found earlier. She could just make out some letters: M-E-L-O-D-Y.

"What is this? My name is on here," she said, surprised. She opened the shell, and out poured a brilliant blue light and beautiful music that sounded somehow familiar. Melody watched as scenes of underwater life appeared: Atlantica, merpeople . . .

Ariel snapped the shell shut. "*Where* did you get this?" she asked, shocked. "You went over the wall, didn't you? You *know* you're not allowed in the sea."

"But why?" asked Melody. "And why does this necklace have my name on it?"

Ariel didn't answer her. "I want you never to go out there again. It's dangerous in the sea."

"How would you know?" asked Melody. "You've never even been in it!" Grabbing the necklace, she ran out of the room.

Ariel and Eric decided Melody should be told the truth. They would tell their daughter about how Ariel had once been a mermaid and how dangerous Morgana was.

Melody sneaked out of the castle and went down to the beach outside the seawall.

"Young lady, just where do you think you're going?" asked Sebastian.

"This necklace means something," said Melody. "If no one's going to tell me, I'm going to find out for myself." More determined than ever, she started rowing out to sea.

Chapter Six

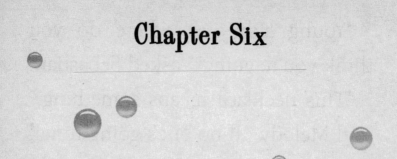

In a cold, dark ice cave, Morgana sat watching Melody's every move in her icy crystal ball.

"Undertow!" Morgana said to her tiny shark, whom King Triton had shrunk to the size of a guppy years earlier. "I shall grant her her wish, and she'll grant mine!"

She ordered the grumpy Undertow to bring Melody to her. Undertow swam off to meet Melody, with Morgana's evil manta rays, Cloak and Dagger, at his side.

Melody's worried parents had searched the entire castle for her. Then they found Sebastian babbling to himself by the seawall.

"All right, you must remain calm. This is not your fault," said Sebastian, talking to himself. Then he screamed, "Melody's gone!"

"Gone? Gone where?" asked a very panicked Ariel.

"Out to da sea," Sebastian pointed with his claw.

"What do you mean?" asked Ariel. "Where could she be going?"

They set off in their ship at once. King Triton had appeared and was ready to help find Melody.

The sea king said, "Everything's going to be all right. We have search parties scouring the ocean. I'm going to join them now myself."

"I should have known I couldn't keep Melody from the sea," said Ariel. "It's a part of her and a part of me. I have to go."

Eric hugged Ariel. "Bring her home,"

he said. And with that, King Triton raised his trident, and with a magnificent beam of light, transformed Ariel into a mermaid once again.

Undertow found Melody in her boat and lured her into Morgana's trap.

"Can Morgana tell me what this locket means and why it has my name on it?" Melody begged.

"Oh sure, kid," chuckled Undertow. "Morgana's the best. She'll help you."

Cloak and Dagger began towing Melody's boat farther and farther out to sea toward Morgana's hideout.

Chapter Seven

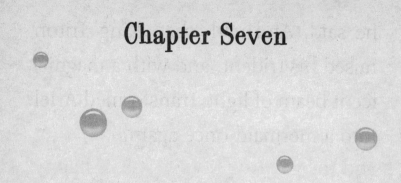

Melody and Undertow soon arrived at the ice cave where Morgana had her hideout. "I was hoping you could tell me about this pendant. Why does it have my name on it?" Melody blurted out. "My mother wouldn't tell me."

"Deep down, you know you

weren't meant to be a lowly *human*. What you are is something far more enchanting—a mermaid," Morgana said as she opened the shell pendant and the glowing bubble full of happy underwater scenes appeared once more.

"A *mermaid*?" said Melody. "But it's not possible."

"One drop of this potion and *badda beem badda boom*—you're in fin city!" said Morgana, holding the bottle in front of Melody. "Come, my darling, your destiny awaits you." She poured out a drop of potion, and a small tornado of snowflakes started to swirl around Melody. She was lifted up, and in a flash, her legs were transformed into a tail.

"I don't believe it! I'm a mermaid!" exclaimed Melody joyfully. Melody spun up, down, and around through the water, trying out her new fins.

She was so happy she actually hugged Morgana.

Then Morgana explained that the potion would not last.

"Please! I don't want to go back to being an ordinary girl," said Melody. "Isn't there *some* way I can stay a mermaid?"

"Well," said Morgana. "I *could* make

Ariel can't wait to introduce Melody to her grandfather, King Triton.

King Triton shows Ariel and Melody visions of life
under the sea in Atlantica, the home of the merpeople.

Twelve-year-old Melody doing what she loves best:
swimming in the ocean, doing somersaults!

Princess Melody feels awkward at her own ball,
until a handsome boy asks her to dance.

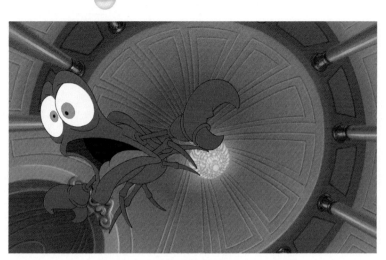

Sebastian takes a flying leap at the ball!

Melody is missing, and her parents are very worried!

The evil Morgana has Melody in her clutches.
"You weren't meant to be a lowly *human*. What you
are is something far more enchanting—a mermaid."

Flounder's boys play a game of underwater Kick the Clam.

Melody feels truly free as a mermaid.

She is finally out of her shell!

Melody steals the trident for Morgana, not realizing
that it belongs to her very own grandfather!

"All the power of the seven seas is at my command!" cries Morgana.

Tip and Dash have a tricky decision to make:
help save Melody, or live a long, healthy life—as cowardly worms!

King Triton points the trident at Morgana.
"Never again will you or yours threaten my family!" he declares.

Ariel tells Melody that she loves her
whether she is a mermaid or a girl.

Melody helps unite sea folk and land folk.
"There's plenty of water for everyone!"

the spell last longer if I had my magic trident. But it was stolen years ago by a deranged kleptomaniac named King Triton, and there's no one to get it back for me."

"If I got back your magic trident, would you make me a mermaid forever?" asked Melody.

Morgana promised that she would. Then she showed Melody the map of Atlantica and where to find King Triton.

Chapter Eight

Not too far away, a small but feisty penguin named Tip slid across the ice with his walrus pal, Dash. Tip shouted, "Mightier than a hurricane! Braver than a killer whale! It's the fearless adventurers, Titanic Tip and his trusty sidekick, Dash!"

This was mostly an act. The two

friends were really kind of scaredy-cats. The other penguins and walruses liked to make fun of their brave boasts.

"Go ahead!" yelled Tip. "Laugh your stinkin' tuxedos off! We'll show you!"

Nearby, Melody was lost. Her luck only got worse when a whale swimming beneath her let loose a gigantic sneeze. Before she knew it, Melody was blown up out of the water and into the air. She landed on the iceberg, right in front of Tip and Dash.

"Excuse me," Melody said to the

frightened penguin and walrus. "You don't have to be scared of me."

"Scared? Who said anything about being scared?" said Tip.

"This here's Tip and I'm Dash," said the walrus.

"Do either of you know how to get to Atlantica?" asked Melody. "I don't have much time."

"Why do you wanna go to Atlantica?" asked Dash.

"I have to get something that was stolen. If I don't, I'll turn back into a human," said Melody sadly.

"We'll take you," said Dash.

"We will?" asked Tip.

Dash took Tip aside. "She's a damsel in distress. It's our big chance!" The friends knew that helping to save Melody was a brave thing to do.

Tip agreed. "I can't believe I'm doing this. Somebody stop me!" he shouted. And the three new friends swam off toward Atlantica.

Chapter Nine

Swimming fast, Ariel finally reached her old home. She caught a glimpse of a small striped fish she thought she recognized. She grabbed him and hugged him. The fish yelled in fright, "DAAAAAAADDDDDY!"

From behind the reef appeared Flounder, all grown up, four times bigger than Ariel remembered.

"Ariel!" cried Flounder.

"Sorry," said Ariel to the little fish. Then she turned to his dad and said, "You're not a guppy anymore." She and Flounder hugged happily. "Flounder, I really need your help," she pleaded.

"Wild sea horses couldn't stop me," answered Flounder, as they swam off to find Melody.

On the other side of Atlantica, Melody, Dash, and Tip arrived. "I knew it! It *is* real," cried Melody. The underwater city that lay before them was more amazing than Melody's wildest dreams.

They hid inside the palace, under a table, and watched King Triton. "He looks sad," said Melody. "He doesn't look like a thief."

"They never do," replied Tip.

When no one was looking, Melody grabbed the golden trident. Her shell necklace fell off, but there was no time to pick it up.

The three friends swam away at top speed.

"Yes! We did it!" cried Tip, bursting with excitement. He and Dash gave each other high fives.

But Melody's mood suddenly changed as they drew closer to her home. "All this time, Atlantica was never that far away," said Melody, with a sigh.

"*This* is your home?" asked Dash, pointing toward the castle.

"It used to be," Melody said sadly.

Seconds later, King Triton, Ariel, and Flounder swam into the throne room only to discover that the trident was missing.

"Melody!" exclaimed Ariel, finding the necklace.

"Morgana! If she gets her hands on

my trident . . ." the king started, very angry.

"Go ahead, crack me open. Make a crab cake outta me, sire!" begged Sebastian. But King Triton was too upset about his granddaughter to pay any attention to him.

Ariel caught sight of Cloak and Dagger. She and Flounder took off after them. She had a hunch that the two manta rays would lead them right to Morgana.

Chapter Ten

Clasping the trident, Melody swam swiftly toward Morgana's icy fortress. Tip caught a ride on Dash. The friends were inseparable. That is, until Tip and Dash caught a glimpse of Undertow. Undertow might have been the size of a guppy, but he still looked a lot like a shark. Tip and

Dash had run away and were out of sight before Melody even noticed Undertow.

"Hey, you got it!" said Undertow, wearing a wicked grin. "Sweetheart, you're my new hero. Let's go. It's time for some magic!"

"Oh, there you are, darling!" Morgana exclaimed when they entered the icy hideout. "Now, if you'll just hand over the . . ."

But before she could finish, Ariel and Flounder burst into the hideout.

"Melody, don't!" shouted Ariel.

"Mom?! You're a *mermaid*!?" asked a confused Melody. "All this time, and you never told me?"

"Please, give the trident to me, Melody," pleaded Ariel.

"No, hand it to me!" yelled Morgana. "She's the one who lied to you all these years!"

"Melody," said Ariel, "if there was one thing in my life I could do over, I . . ."

But it was too late. Melody passed the trident to Morgana.

"All the power of the seven seas is at my command!" cried Morgana. Thunder and lightning crackled around the cave as she held the trident.

"Hello! Can we get with the program? It's still a small world down here!" said Undertow, who couldn't stand being small.

But Morgana was busy. She grabbed Ariel with one tentacle and gagged her with another. When Flounder and Melody tried to interfere, she brushed them aside. "Melody, all these years, your mummy was only trying to protect you from *moi*," Morgana said. "And Little Melody's been a very naughty girl, stealing from her own grandfather!"

"My grandfather?" asked Melody.

"King Triton, ruler of Atlantica and commander in chief of all the oceans," said Morgana with a wicked laugh. "Until a certain little thief came along!"

With that, she threw Melody and Flounder into an ice cave and sealed them in.

Chapter Eleven

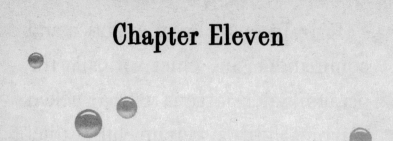

Morgana grew larger and rose up through her cracking iceberg fortress to the surface of the ocean. There, she saw Prince Eric heading toward her on his ship. With a *kaboom!* she tore his ship in half. He scrambled toward shore and collapsed unconscious.

The ocean rumbled and churned as

a legion of mermen who were ready for battle began to rise up from the sea. King Triton had tracked down Morgana—but was it too late?

King Triton appeared and said, "Release my daughter, surrender my granddaughter, and I shall spare you."

"Oh," replied Morgana coldly. "What are you gonna do? Throw the crab at me?" She kept blasting away with the trident, and no one could stop her.

Tiny Undertow appeared at her side once again. "Now look at me! I'm BAIT!"

Morgana finally zapped him, restoring him to his enormous shark size.

Meanwhile, back in the ice cave, Melody watched in horror as her fins turned back into legs. She was human again and could no longer breathe under water. Time was running out! Soon she would be trapped forever in the icy tomb!

On an iceberg above, Tip and Dash debated about what they should do. "On the one hand, we can live a long, healthy life—as *cowardly worms*," said Tip.

"Melody could be in trouble and

may really need our help," added Dash.

Tip and Dash were swimming to the rescue when they spotted Undertow. He looked big and hungry. Dash jumped on his back while Tip swam off to find Melody, but Undertow chased right after Tip. By covering Undertow's eyes, Dash made him crash right through an ice wall at full speed! *Ouch!* This knocked him out and at the same time, freed Melody and Flounder.

Tip and Dash swam straight to the surface with Melody. When they placed her on the ice, she gasped for breath. They were real heroes, after all.

Chapter Twelve

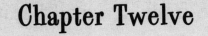

Melody watched in horror as Morgana screamed, "Fools! I have the trident now, and all the creatures of the sea are in my power. Bow down to me!"

Tip, Dash, and the rest were unable to resist her command. One by one, the sea creatures bowed. But Melody was free from her spell because she was human. Right then, she knew it was up to her, and her alone, to fight Morgana.

Even King Triton felt the force of Morgana's power. "That's it, Triton. Bow down before me!" screeched Morgana. Ariel bowed down as well.

Slowly and carefully, Melody snuck up the icy cliff, past Morgana's slimy, slithering tentacles. Then, in a flash, Melody surprised Morgana, snatched the trident, and threw it to King Triton, shouting, "Grandfather, I think this belongs to you!"

King Triton pointed the trident at

Morgana. He declared, "Never again will you or yours threaten my family!"

Morgana was instantly frozen in a block of ice and sunk far beneath the sea.

Melody hugged Ariel and Eric. "I'm sorry, Mother," said Melody.

"No, sweetie, we're sorry," said Ariel. "We should have told you the truth."

"I didn't mean to hurt anyone," said Melody. "I just hoped I'd be a better mermaid than a girl."

"Oh, Melody, it doesn't matter if you have fins *or* feet. We love you for who you are on the inside—our very brave daughter," said Ariel proudly.

"Just like your mother," added King Triton.

"Oh, Grandfather!" exclaimed Melody as she hugged her grandfather for the first time.

"Because you're my granddaughter, I'm giving you a most precious gift. A choice: you can come to Atlantica with me or you can return to your home on land. It's up to you," said the king.

It was the hardest decision Melody had ever had to make. She had loved being a mermaid, but she loved life with her family, too.

"I have a better idea," Melody said.

Back at the castle, sea folk and land folk alike cheered as Melody blasted the seawall to tiny bits.

"Come on in!" cried Melody, performing a beautiful cannonball dive off Mermaid Rock. "There's plenty of water for everyone!"

Are you a Disney Princess?

Do you want to be like Belle or Ariel? Snow White or Jasmine? Pocahontas or Sleeping Beauty?

Check out Disney's Princesses Pull-Out Posters and Game Cards Book

Plaster your bedroom walls with posters of Cinderella, Snow White, Sleeping Beauty.
Get together with your friends and play the Princess card games.

A must for all future Disney Princesses!

AVAILABLE OCTOBER 2000

Look for this exciting title from Disney Interactive

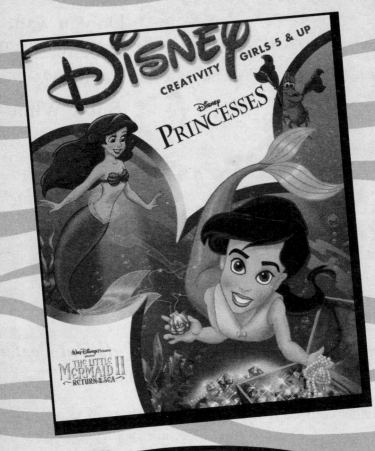

Get ready for a
Splashtacular adventure!

www.disneyinteractive.com

HOWDY, PARDNERS!

Your favorite characters are back in this new rootin' tootin' highfalutin' paperback series.

WOODY'S ROUNDUP #1:
Showdown at the Okey Dokey Corral

WOODY'S ROUNDUP #2:
Giddy-Up Ghost Town

WOODY'S ROUNDUP #3:
Ride 'Em Rodeo!

WOODY'S ROUNDUP #4:
Fool's Gold

THESE BOOKS ARE SIDE-WINDING TO A CORRAL NEAR YOU

SEPTEMBER 2000

DINOSAUR READ-ALOUD
STORYBOOK
0-7364-1000-7

DINOSAUR: ZINI'S
BIG ADVENTURE
0-7868-4408-6

You loved
the MOVIES,

NOW RELIVE
the MAGIC

TOY STORY II
READ-ALOUD STORYBOOK
0-7364-0151-2

TOY STORY II: REX TO THE RESCUE
DISNEY CHAPTER BOOK
0-7868-4288-1

A BUG'S LIFE
CLASSIC STORYBOOK
1-57082-979-9

A BUG'S LIFE: FLICK TO THE RESCUE
DISNEY CHAPTER BOOK
0-7868-4251-2

WITH THESE
MOVIE
TIE-IN TITLES.

TARZAN READ-ALOUD
STORYBOOK
0-7364-0047-8

MULAN CLASSIC
STORYBOOK
1-57082-864-4

MULAN: MUSHU'S STORY
DISNEY CHAPTER BOOK
0-7868-4225-3

AVAILABLE NOW

Michelle Kwan, the internationally renowned figure skater, presents

MICHELLE KWAN PRESENTS *Skating* Dreams

A new paperback book series about Lauren Wing, a young figure skater, whose hopes and fears, thrills and heartbreaks, closely parallel Michelle's own experiences.

SKATING DREAMS #1:
The Turning Point

SKATING DREAMS #2:
Staying Balanced

SKATING DREAMS #3:
Skating Backwards
Coming September 2000

SKATING DREAMS #4:
Champion's Luck
Coming November 2000

HYPERION BOOKS FOR CHILDREN